I Don't Want to Want to Go to School!

Translation copyright © 2009 by Random House, Inc.
Translated by Whitney Stahlberg

Published in the United States by Random House Children's Books,
a division of Random House, Inc., New York.
Originally published in France as *Je veux pas aller à l'école* by l'école des loisirs, Paris, in 2007.
Copyright © 2007 by l'école des loisirs, Paris.

Random House and colophon are registered trademarks of Random House, Inc.

Visit us on the Web!
www.randomhouse.com/kids

Educators and librarians, for a variety of teaching tools, visit us at
www.randomhouse.com/teachers

Library of Congress Cataloging-in-Publication Data
Blake, Stephanie.
[Je veux pas aller à l'école. English]
I don't want to go to school! / Stephanie Blake. — 1st American ed.
p. cm.
Summary: Simon the rabbit does not want to go to his first day of school,
but by the time his mother comes to take him home,
he is having such a good time that he does not want to leave.
ISBN 978-0-375-85688-4 (trade) — ISBN 978-0-375-95688-1 (lib. bdg.)
[1. First day of school—Fiction. 2. Schools—Fiction. 3. Rabbits—Fiction.]
I. Title. II. Title: I do not want to go to school!
PZ7.B565 Iaf 2009 [E]—dc22
2008011256

MANUFACTURED IN MALAYSIA
10 9 8 7 6 5 4 3 2 1
First American Edition

I Don't Want to Go to School!

Written and illustrated by

Stephanie Blake

Random House 🏠 New York

There once was a mischievous little rabbit named Simon. With a big smile, his mother told him, "Tomorrow is your first day of school, my dear!"

Simon answered, "No way!"

His father told him, "But, my little rabbit, you're going to learn the alphabet at school."

Simon answered, "No way!"

That night, Simon couldn't
fall asleep.

"Mommy!!!"

"I don't want to go to school!"
Simon told his mother.

She tucked him in and comforted
him. "You are the bravest little rabbit.
You are my *super* rabbit."

Simon answered, "No way!"

The next morning, Simon's mother told him, "Hurry up and eat your breakfast, my little rabbit. It's almost time to leave for school."

Simon answered, "No way!"

On the way, Simon's father said, "You're going to make friends at school. And you're going to learn lots of new things. I am so proud of you. You are my BIG rabbit."

Simon answered, "No way!"

Outside the school, Simon's father hugged him tight and said, "Have a great day, my dear. I'm going to leave you now."

In a tiny little voice, Simon answered, "No way!"

At school, Simon did many
things. . . .

First he cried.

Then he drew.

At recess, he played.

In the cafeteria, he ate chocolate mousse.

Then he rested.

In the afternoon, he played the drums.

And at 3:30, when Simon's mother arrived to pick him up, she said, "It's time to go home, my dear."
Simon answered . . .

"NO WAY!"